The Pout-Pout Fish

in the Big-Big Dark

Deborah Diesen

Pictures by Dan Hanna

Farrar Straus Giroux
New York

For Tobin
—D.D.
For Mom, Dad, family, friends, and Jennifer
—D.H.

Text copyright © 2010 by Deborah Diesen
Pictures copyright © 2010 by Dan Hanna
All rights reserved
Color separations by Embassy Graphics Ltd.
Printed in China by RR Donnelley Asia Printing Solutions Ltd.,
Dongguan City, Guangdong Province
Designed by Jay Colvin
First edition, 2010
20 19 18 17 16 15 14 13 12 11

poutpoutfish.com
mackids.com

Library of Congress Cataloging-in-Publication Data
Diesen, Deborah.
    The pout-pout fish in the big-big dark / Deborah Diesen ; pictures by Dan Hanna.— 1st ed.
        p.   cm.
    Summary: Mr. Fish feels nervous venturing deep in the sea to look for Ms. Clam's lost pearl until Miss
Shimmer helps him conquer his fear of the dark.
    ISBN: 978-0-374-30798-1
    [1. Stories in rhyme.   2. Fishes—Fiction.   3. Marine animals—Fiction.   4. Fear of the dark—Fiction.
5. Lost and found possessions—Fiction.]   I. Hanna, Dan, ill.   II. Title.

PZ8.3.D565Po 2010
[E]—dc22
                                                                2009013601

A doozie of a drowsy
Made Ms. Clam yawn.
Then a big current *whooshed*
And her pearl was GONE!

Mr. Fish swam forth.
"Ms. Clam, don't weep!
I will find your pearl—
That's a promise I'll keep!"

He swooped through the water,
Swishing close to the sand,
And he eyed every inch
Of the busy bottom land.

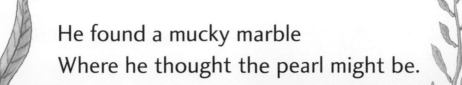

He found a mucky marble
Where he thought the pearl might be.

Then a hidden voice whispered,
"It's further out to sea!"

So he swam a little deeper,
Where the light grew dimmer.
As his heart flit-fluttered,
Mr. Fish grew grimmer.

He kept on searching
All along the ocean floor,

Through a reef, through a wreck,
Swimming far from the shore.

Mr. Fish felt a pout-pout
Poach on his hope.

Then the whisper from before
Said, "It's down beyond the slope!"

So he swam a little deeper,
Where the light grew dimmer.
As his heart flit-fluttered,
Mr. Fish grew grimmer.

"I'm **FAST** as a sailfish,

I'm **STRONG** as a shark,

I'm **SMART** as a dolphin . . .

But I'm **scared of the dark.**"

A whirl of wriggly worms
Made a search-team swirl,
And they helped with the hunt
For the yawn-gone pearl.

But nothing was discovered.
Mr. Fish felt despair!
Then that soft voice whispered,
"In the trench—check *there*."

So he swam a little deeper,
Where the light grew dimmer.
As his heart flit-fluttered,
Mr. Fish grew grimmer.

SUCKERS HERE!

REST STOP!

OPEN ALL NIGHT

Famous CAVE of MYSTERY

Come on in!

FREE FOOD

FUN and GAMES! In Here!

SCENIC ROUTE This Way

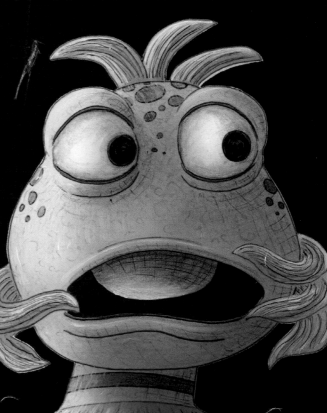

"I *won't* keep swimming
In this heap-deep black!
I know I made a promise,
But this fish is headin' back!"

Then a whisper, now familiar,
Whisked away his dread.
"You can *do* it, Mr. Fish,"
Her sweet voice said.

Though there wasn't any light,
Not the smallest, slim glimmer,
Mr. Fish felt braver . . .

Cheered on by Miss Shimmer:

"Two are **FASTER** than a sailfish,

Two are **STRONGER** than a shark,

Two are **SMARTER** than a dolphin . . .

Two are **BIGGER** than the dark!"

So they swam down together,
Holding fin to fin,
When suddenly,
Amazingly . . .

LIGHT SHONE IN!

Mr. Fish said, "Yes!"
Miss Shimmer shouted, "Yay!"
"There's Ms. Clam's pearl!
Hooray! Hoo-*ray*!!!"

They **SMOOCHED** Mr. Lantern.

Then they smiled as they swam,
Weaving back through the water
To a happy Ms. Clam.

The whole gang gathered,
Feeling glorious and proud,
And they swam in a circle
As they sang out loud:

"The ocean is wide,
And the ocean is deep,
But *friends help friends*—
That's a promise we keep."

We are bigger,

Yes, BIGGER,

Always big,

BIG,

BIGGER,

Than the dark!